Meeting of the Mustangs

Cathy Kennedy

In 1971, President Richard Nixon signed into effect The
Wild Free-Roaming Horses and Burros Act. The act
covered the management, protection and study of
"unbranded and unclaimed horses and burros on public
lands in the United States."

In no way does the author suggest or condone the capturing
of any wild horse. Wild mustangs may be adopted through
The Bureau of Land Management.
https://www.blm.gov/adoptahorse/

This book is also available as an ebook. Please visit
Amazon or your favorite online ebook retailer for more
information.

*****

He didn't see the butterfly that flew past his nose, but he did see its shadow. He got up from his silly coltish position and began to chase it. For the three months of his life so far, he had always loved to chase shadows. He would chase bird shadows, butterfly shadows, even things as silly as shadows of tall flowers blowing in the wind. He often caught up with them, too, but he could never figure out why he couldn't keep ahold of them. It was just too much for his young mind, despite the fact that he was only a horse.

The reason he could catch up with them was because he was fast --- very fast. In fact, he was much faster than any of the other three- and four-month-old mustangs in the band. He had been born three months before, to a big, beautiful chestnut mare and his sire, who was also large. He was colored like his sire – pitch black.

Only hours before, the big mountain lion had attacked again. The horses were peacefully grazing when the stealthy cat had dropped from a tree and onto the black colt's unsuspecting father. Hearing his screams of distress and fearing for the safety of the band, the lead mare had signaled for them to flee. Panicked, they left the scene at full gallop, leaving the unfortunate stallion to fight the cat alone.

Although the mountain lion had not pursued them, the mares and young horses ran a great distance, the mares pushing the younger ones to keep pace with them. When the young horses could go no further, they had finally slowed and come to rest, the lead mare intently looking in every direction to make certain that the predator had not followed them.

His sides still heaving, the black colt had seen that his sire was no longer with them, and he gazed up at his mother, looking for reassurance. She nickered and nuzzled him gently.

The alpha mare, a wise old palomino, had known that she needed to move the band to a safer location. She

1

calmed the horses, got them focused, and seemed to be accounting for each horse's presence. When she was satisfied, they moved westward, stopping only to graze and to allow the foals to nurse. For the next several days, the little colt stayed beside his mother almost constantly.

There was an older colt in the band who had been permitted to remain with them since his birth. While he was far from mature, in the days that followed, he seemed to recognize his newly acquired position and did his best to assist with the group's protection.

One afternoon, while they were grazing in the middle of a large series of lush, green meadows, the little colt sensed something wrong and gave an excited whinny to show it. None of the other horses paid any attention to him. At this, he began to carry on while keeping a lookout for the danger he sensed. Then, the leader saw them. Men! She could see a small group of them on foot in the distance and they seemed to be moving away from the horses, but she knew that they still could not afford to take any chances on an encounter with these unpredictable beings. It wasn't often that they saw men, but they had learned that it was always best to avoid any contact with them.

The sun was high in the sky when the band took off to get away from these dreaded creatures. Their fear of men had been handed down to them from their ancestors, who were constantly being hunted by them. They continued to move west, the older colt keeping his place in the rear of the group and urging them forward. When the men were no longer to be seen, the lead mare halted and gathered the mares and foals together. She knew that they were safe now but she also knew that they could not go back to that wonderful paradise.

She was satisfied with the area in which they had stopped; except for the fact that there were no shade trees as close by, it provided a swiftly-flowing stream. While the adult horses drank from the stream, the young foals waited patiently until it was their turn for some milk. As the young colt drank, a feeling of peace came over him, for he was beside his mother.

~~~~~

Blood and sweat trickled down the little colt's heaving sides. They had run for a long time. The mountain lion had struck again, but this time gotten no meat. It had been the little colt who had given the warning signal again. He had much better senses than any of the other horses in the band, even though he was one of the youngest.

The mountain lion must have tracked them. Now, they all knew that they must keep moving and never stop for long periods of time until they were sure of safety. As the little colt drank the sweet milk from his mother, she cleaned his wounds and comforted him.

They passed out of Kansas and into Colorado. The mountain lion was gone now but they still had many other worries.

Most importantly, they had to find some good ground suitable for foaling, as some mares were soon due. They hadn't gone too far when they reached some ground almost like the last, except that there was a great expanse of grassland surrounded by majestic old trees. It was almost as if someone had planted them there years before, but no one had. There was a beautiful stream, thick grass, and the trees for shade. It would be suitable until danger arose.

Late that night, a chestnut mare gave birth to a little filly. The older foals were especially curious, stretching their necks and competing for the best view of the newcomer. The little foal was on its long legs within hours and scampering around to meet its new family.

During the next week, six other mares foaled, but only four of the six foals lived. Two mares had had problems and while they did everything they could, their babies did not survive. There was a sense of urgency between the foaling mares and the leader, and while she tried to help, the wise old palomino allowed the foals' mothers to mourn their losses.

The energetic youngsters kept them all entertained and alert and there was no more trouble; the grass was good and the water plentiful. The little colt took on a bulkier outline and was soon mixing grass in with his diet.

Late one night as the horses were grazing, the leader came upon some fresh bear tracks. She sensed danger as did the other horses. The little black colt was sleeping when the cry of danger came from the leader. He awoke instantly and was beside his mother in seconds.

The black bear dropped to all fours and began to chase the band. He got his prize --- the little black colt! They both fought savagely, the little colt crying out in pain and anger. He saw his mother coming. The bear looked up and saw flashing hooves not far above his face. Her flailing hooves came down but missed the target as the bear rolled to the side. The big horse rose again and came crashing down on its head and chest. Both bear and colt lay still.

~~~~~~

As the little colt lay there, his mother smelled him over. She knew that she had killed the bear. Anger filled her, and she began to lick the colt's wounds. Slowly, he opened his eyes and looked at her. Though he was bleeding and very weak, he got up and walked slowly to the creek. There, he lay down and the water washing over him cleaned his wounds. His strength slowly came back and he wearily got up and went to his mother, who was grazing close by. He began to drink and this put new strength into him, though he was still unsteady. Had it not been for his mother's constant attention, he surely would have died. She continued to attend to his wounds and give him plenty to drink.

The cold nights gradually got warmer as the days wore on. They had not changed location since the bear had been killed and there had been no more trouble.

The little colt's wounds healed very slowly and he was weak from his loss of blood. As the days grew warmer and his wounds got better, he began to romp in the grass with the other foals. He was the only one who chased shadows, though.

One warm, clear evening, while the colts and fillies were playing a nippy game, they wandered a bit far from the other horses. None of them really noticed until it was too late. The youngsters were a good distance away when a large, chestnut mare stopped grazing and swung her head up in alarm. When she saw that the foals were missing, she called out a loud cry of distress. The leader looked up in surprise. She was ashamed at not being the first to notice and to be the one that had let the young horses wander astray.

The colts and fillies had come to a narrow crevice in some rocks and were curious to see what was inside. The little black colt went in first. He did not see the pair of golden eyes that were staring at him from up high. As he walked on farther, the eyes dipped down and the owner of them made a loud fluttering sound. This petrified the foals, but they were too scared to move. They stood still as statues as the owl made its way out of the rocks and rose into the sky.

After some time, the black colt turned the others around and they made their way to the exit of the crevice. As they approached the opening, they looked straight into the eyes of an angry white mare. She gave each of them a sharp nip as they ran out of the opening and past her. This was to teach them to never do anything like that again. As they returned to the band, anxious mothers trotted out to meet their foals. Each of the sucklings drank and drank, and they settled down to rest for the night.

The next morning, the little black colt was awakened by the howl of a coyote. It was very far off in the distance and didn't pose any danger. While the little colt and other young horses in the band were not off their mothers' milk, they were starting to enjoy the springtime flowers and tender new grass. A rabbit hopped off in the distance, giving the whole scene a sort of peacefulness.

The colts and fillies romped in the grass in the Colorado sunshine. This time, they did not wander, as they could still feel the sharp little nips that the mare had given them the day before. Today, the black colt felt a bit lazy. The sun did this to him sometimes. He didn't even feel like chasing any shadows. He quietly moved off to the side and lay down to watch the others play.

~~~~~~

The grass got greener as the days got warmer and the days seemed longer to the colt. He was still the same color as the day he was born and had no markings at all.

One day as the little colt and his cousin were romping playfully in the grass, they came across a strange object lying in the grass. Fear rose up inside them as they sniffed at it and detected the smells of man and something very pungent; little did they know that it was a bullet casing. They ran back to their mothers and drank nervously.

One evening not long afterwards, as they were grazing, a

piercing gunshot rang through the air and the leader suddenly dropped to the ground. As the little colt looked at her, she appeared to be helpless. She was an experienced and very wise mare and he had never known her to be this way. The young men approached, laughing, and the other horses fled. The older colt also kept his distance, but refused to back off too far as he knew that they were his responsibility.

The men came closer. There were three of them and, as they neared the mare, the little colt, who had been expecting her to get up, also fled.

"We better get outta here," exclaimed the young man who was holding the gun. As they leaned over the mare, she suddenly got up, unhurt, and the shocked young men had no choice but to run. The young man holding the gun stumbled over his own feet and dropped it in his effort to retreat. The angry mare whinnied and chased him first. She was having fun now. One of the boys was practically howling and appeared to be headed for a tree.

Not sure what to make of the situation, the rest of the horses watched from a distance as the old mare eliminated the danger. It wasn't long before she cantered over to them, whinnied, and seemed to say *All done! Follow me!* and they proudly followed her into the foothills.

Miles away was another band of horses that was slowly making its way closer to the black colt and his band. The large group of healthy mares and foals had no stallion with them; he had been killed by the same mountain lion that seemed intent on stalking the colt's band. Three days later, the mares and foals caught up with the colt's band and the leader willingly accepted the new mares and foals. Three of the mares in each band were due to foal any day.

Five of them came that night; two Appaloosas, one chestnut and two bays. The sixth came the following evening. He was a beautiful strawberry roan. Of the six new foals, there were four fillies and two colts. The band was now very large, due to the new mares and foals. The leader knew that she had a big responsibility now and she knew how to handle it.

That night, there was a powerful rainstorm that made the nearby creek flow swifter than it ever had. The Colorado mountains were beautiful, and as the black colt gazed at them, a coyote howled in the distance.

The following weeks brought cooler weather, which made travel much easier for the horses; they could travel longer distances without having to stop as often to rest and cool themselves. When they weren't suckling, grazing or napping, the younger horses would spend most days playing. *Catch me if you can!* they seemed to say to one another as they played what appeared to be their version of a game of Tag.

Soon, they began to put on weight and their coats became thick and fuzzy in preparation for the upcoming winter. When the snows came, the little ones were entranced with it. How they loved the snow! They would run and jump and chase each other, their breath coming out of their noses like puffy white clouds.

They watched the adult horses and learned how to push the snow on the ground aside in order to find the grass underneath. When they were lucky, the horses were able to find areas of naturally protected ground which had received significantly less accumulation of snow, and the grass was much easier to find in these areas. There were also small shrubs, bushes, and other foliage that provided them with food. They usually had no trouble finding running water in streams and rivers, but would resort to eating snow on occasion if they had to.

Fortunately, it turned out to be a relatively mild winter and their losses were minimal. When the sun began to melt the ice and snow and the days became longer, the horses began to shed their winter coats, pulling out the now-unneeded hair by rubbing against trees or rolling on the ground. None of them were unhappy when the snow finally disappeared and the new grass began to emerge from the soggy ground.

~~~~~

With the arrival of spring, the colt was eating full rations of grass and his mother was completely dry. The strawberry roan foal and the black colt were inseparable buddies and were now romping in the spring sunshine. The black colt was chasing the shadows of some geese flying overhead and the little strawberry roan was eyeing him uncertainly, trying to keep up with him.

The black colt became tired and began to graze and the little roan soon caught up with him. That's when it happened. The roan looked around and saw that they were all alone. He let out a scream of terror and the little colt flung his head up. They ran in every direction, but the band was nowhere to be found.

The sun was setting low as the two frightened colts searched. The roan was in need of food, and the black colt tried to encourage him to eat grass. The black colt could now live without the protection of his mother, for he was almost a yearling, but the little roan needed his mother.

They continued to search for the band and it was midway through the next day when the little roan collapsed. He was in desperate need of milk. The black colt didn't know what to do for his friend. For some time, he continued to search, but was unable to locate the band. Finally, he returned to the starving animal. Then, because he didn't know what else to do, he lay down close to the foal and tried to comfort it.

Each day the roan was getting skinnier. Each day the colt would go out and look for the band but always returned to the little roan colt. One evening, when the black colt got back from searching, he saw the little roan lying even more still than it ever had. The colt walked over to it slowly, afraid of the truth; but it was true, the roan had died. He walked away sadly, knowing that he need not return again. Now he was free to wander as far as he could to look for the band, but, after many weeks of searching, he finally gave up.

~~~~~

The colt was now a yearling and was filling out at a very fast rate. He stood a little over twelve hands and had beautiful sloping shoulders, a short, but full back, arched neck, and a chiseled head. He was still the same pitch black as the day he was born and always would be.

As he roamed the fields one afternoon, lonely and sad, he detected the scent of something he knew and hated. He looked toward the horizon and saw the mountain lion slinking toward him. His first impulse was to run. Instead, he decided to defend himself by fighting the cat, in a courageous effort to eliminate this constant threat.

He stood his ground as it came closer, a low growl escaping its parted jaws. The yearling's body was tense with fear and trepidation and he continued to fight the urge to run. The big cat stopped moving, and, keeping its eyes fixed on the yearling, crouched down lower to the ground before sprinting directly at him. The yearling skillfully dodged to the side, but he felt a shot of pain as the cat's claws gouged his left flank. Quickly pivoting his body away from the cat, he backed up as the cat readied itself for a powerful leap. It covered the distance between them with amazing speed and made an attempt at the yearling's throat. Again, the yearling side-stepped its jaws and as the cat was turning back toward him, he leaned forward and gave a massive kick with both hind legs. The mountain lion's head snapped backward and it was thrown off balance. It managed to keep its footing but it was bleeding from a gash just under its jaw. It seemed to be struggling to regain its balance and the yearling took the opportunity to gain an advantage over it. Knowing that it would probably be his only chance and keeping his head protectively lowered, he raced toward the unprepared cat, spun around, and kicked it squarely in the side of the head. There was a loud *snap!* and the cat was actually airborne for a moment before it hit the ground in a heap, its head positioned beside its body at an unnatural angle.

The yearling stood where he was, his sides heaving, and waited to see what the cat would do next. When there was no movement from the dead animal, he cautiously took a few steps forward and looked at it from a short distance. Pleased with what he saw and knowing that he had been very lucky, he turned and quickly trotted away.

~~~~~~

He became accustomed to being alone and tried not to think about his lost band. He was more concerned about the food and water that he had to find in order to stay alive and healthy. He began to take on a new shape; his coat developed a luxurious shine and he was filling out, becoming a handsome horse. He was still the same coal black color and he still loved to chase shadows.

One evening, around dusk, the yearling came upon the remains of a freshly killed fawn. As he investigated the surrounding area, he smelled coyote. He knew that these animals were dangerous and that he must keep moving.

He was being drawn to the east, toward the rising moon. He quickly traversed ever-changing landscapes that included everything from fields and meadows, thick forests, cacti, assorted bodies of water, and very seldom he would see a single house. Whenever he came near these, he sensed danger and passed quickly, keeping his distance from them. He covered a great distance that evening before finally stopping to rest.

The next morning was enough to brighten anyone's spirit, even the yearling's. The sun felt good and there was a gentle breeze from the north. The yearling, feeling better already, trotted briskly down to a nearby stream where he took a good long drink. After this, he grazed for a few hours and then lay down to rest; the morning sun had made him feel tired and lazy. A persistent fly prevented him from dozing and the sun was high in the sky when he instead set out to see if he could find a friend.

That evening, the yearling found a suitable place to rest. He ate and drank very little and soon fell into a deep and contented sleep. When he awoke, it was drizzling. Throughout the next day, it rained harder and harder. The yearling moved under the shelter of some trees and stayed there most of the day, only coming out to eat and drink when necessary. The day passed very slowly and the yearling was glad when the rain finally stopped. He traveled under the stars that night since he had rested most of the day and wasn't the least bit tired.

~~~~~~

Halfway through the night, the yearling rested. He was tiring easily for some reason. The farmhouses that were once so scarce were now coming into view much more often. The yearling knew that this was bad and began traveling south. The following night, he passed out of Colorado and into New Mexico.

The farmhouses were now even more frequent than they had been before he had changed his direction. Wasn't there anywhere he could go without men or wild animals threatening him?

The next morning, as the sun was beginning to make its way over the mountains, he saw a beautiful horse standing not far ahead of him. He raced for it happily, but when he reached the spot where he'd seen it, he was surprised to see nothing! He looked around and saw nothing. He was completely alone. *It couldn't have run away that fast!*

He was so lonely for a friend that he had only imagined it. As he stood there, the wind howled and a chill ran down his spine. He wasn't cold. Slowly, he walked away.

The following night was beautiful. The sky was clear and almost every single star could be seen. He had been traveling southeast for some time and passed into Oklahoma. He was satisfied with his surroundings, having not seen any signs of predators at all. This pleased him and lifted his spirits. He felt very comfortable in this location; it had plenty of thick pastures and a nice, running creek.

One evening as he was grazing, he stepped onto something cold and hard. A split second later, a pair of steel jaws bit into his leg and a shot of pain ran through his entire body. He struggled to free himself, to no avail, and collapsed in an exhausted heap. Throughout the night, he continued to try to escape the enormous pressure and pain being inflicted on his leg. Trying to pull his leg out of the jaws was useless. He licked his wound and, completely worn out, he finally closed his eyes.

In the morning, he was awakened from a light sleep by a fearful sound and a bitter smell. Two men were coming toward him! Terrified, he managed to get up and support his weight on his three good legs. He could no longer feel the pain because his entire leg had gone numb. The men came still closer and the yearling was petrified when they reached him and stood looking at him. One was short and thin; the other, tall and heavy. The thin one spoke first.

"What should we do with it?" he asked the heavy one. His voice was soft and somehow unusually kind to be coming out of a human's mouth. This confused the yearling. He had never known a human to be kind.

"That trap was meant for that dog-gone bear, not a lousy pony!" yelled the heavy one. All good thoughts about humans left him instantly when the yearling heard this man speak.

"I'm sure it wasn't his fault," said the kind one. "What do you say we just leave him go?"

The two were silent for what seemed a long time to the trembling yearling. Then, slowly, the large man walked toward him. The yearling had no idea what the man intended to do to him and he tried to back away, slamming against a tree in his excitement.

"Get back, Joe!" shouted the smaller one.

The large man said nothing, but stopped in his tracks. Slowly, he turned around to the smaller man.

"We'll just leave him here, Ty. After he's rotten, I'll come back for my trap," he said. "Took me two days to make that thing," he grumbled as he began to walk away.

A twisted look showed clearly on the smaller man's face, but he knew that it did no good to argue with big Joe Deery. He reluctantly turned and joined the big man.

~~~~~~

As the men walked away, the yearling thought he smelled the faint aroma of smoke. He was exhausted and closed his eyes. Some time later, he became aware of a crackling sound in the distance and the strong smell of smoke in the air. He turned his head to the left and was terrified at the sight that met his eyes. The once beautiful woods standing in the distance were ablaze!

The yearling fought ferociously to free himself, but the steel jaws that were clamped onto his leg would not let go. The fire crept closer and as it began to run out of trees for fuel it came toward the yearling, gaining speed in the open grassland. The yearling fought savagely at the trap, but it would not give way. His sides were heaving and he could feel his heart pounding in his chest. On the verge of panic, he heard movement coming toward him and swung his head toward the sound to see the kind man who had been there earlier.

"I couldn't bear the thought of you out here all by yourself, and then when old man Higgins started screaming about a fire, I just had to see if you were all right. Now, if you'll just bear with me, I'll get ya outta there," he was saying as he walked very slowly toward the yearling, his voice gentle in spite of the situation; but the yearling could still not trust a man.

He was so tired, though.

The fire continued its smoky race toward them. The man reached the yearling and slowly knelt down beside his shoulder, still talking reassuringly. The yearling sensed that the man was hesitant, but he also knew, somehow, that he was trying to help him. He lay still as the man pried the jaws apart. When they were finally open, the yearling's leg was so numb and he was so stunned that he did not move at all, even as the fire approached them. The man pulled the trap to one side and set it on the ground.

"Now, get on with you! You wanna get burnt?" he said loudly, standing up and lifting an arm in the air. The yearling got up on all four legs, somehow, and hobbled slowly away from the man and the fire. When he turned his head and looked behind him, he saw the man jogging away at an angle, the trap in his hand.

Behind him, over the constant crackling of the fire, the yearling heard the first menacing rumble of thunder. The sky had become an eerie color of mahogany and although the air was still, he could feel the charge in it. A moment later, he felt the first big raindrops on his head and his back and it wasn't long before they were mercilessly drenching him.

He walked on his three good legs, sort of hop-stepping in the downpour, keeping his bad leg off the ground as much as he could. There were times when he needed to place it on the ground to keep himself from sliding off balance in the mud, and it was then that it hurt most. He kept his head down, eyes partially closed against the rain, scanning the landscape for a place to rest. The frequent lightning provided him with glimpses of the terrain ahead and, peering through the raindrops, he saw nothing but grassland. While his body begged him to stop, his instinct told him to continue, and he finally came to a small gathering of trees. He made his way to the nearest tree and got out of the rain. Thoroughly exhausted, he stood still and rested.

He later found a creek nearby and spent much of his time there, resting and allowing the fresh water to cleanse his wound. The weather was excellent and he had no problems with predators. As the days passed, his leg became stronger and healed nicely. He would only have a small scar.

One evening, while he was grazing, he stumbled onto a little doe lying in a ditch by the creek. The yearling did not know what had killed her, but he knew it was time for him to start moving again. He set out at once, making good time as the sun set slowly in the rose-colored sky.

~~~~~~

The following days were joyous for the yearling. The nights cooled as summer turned into fall and most days were still pleasantly warm.

He was constantly moving and rarely stayed in one place for more than two or three days. The leaves were turning from a deep green to lovely shades of different golds and reds, but the yearling hardly noticed this at all. Soon, birds flying south for the winter to come were squawking over his head.

One morning, a bit before sunrise, the yearling was awakened by the feeling of something scraping across his delicate muzzle. He quickly opened his eyes to find that it was only a leaf that had fallen from the tree he had been dozing under. Soon, the trees were shedding them in heaps on the ground. The nights turned much colder and soon it began to flurry, sometimes for days at a time, so that when he walked, the snow crunched beneath his delicate hooves. He did not mind it at all; he loved the snow! He would run and slide in it, throw it up with his nose and hooves and even eat it when he was unable to find water. He especially missed his friends when he was playing in the snow and he wished he knew where to find them.

One morning, after an incredibly cold night, he saw a cottontail rabbit hopping along the top of the snow. The yearling tried to do it, too, but it didn't work; he always fell through the snow! He attempted all morning and after a frustrated whinny, he realized that he was very tired. He made his way through the snow until he came to his favorite feeding area, which was wearing very thin. He scraped some snow away and began to nibble at the brown grass that was beneath it. It was then he decided that it was time to move on again.

The heaviest snows came early in the winter; while there was some drifting later on, the snowfall was relatively light and made it much easier for the yearling to find food.

April arrived and there was no more snow, only wetness. The melting snow ran down the mountains and hills like rivers and when the temperature went below freezing, it was very hard to walk on the solid ice, and even harder to break through it in order to get food. But, miraculously, the yearling made it through the winter alone. He was a strong horse, like his parents had been.

Before long, green sprouts shot from the tree branches like miniature torpedoes stopped in mid-air. All the snow was gone and the ground was very soggy. The green grass came into the world slowly but surely and the yearling was very glad for that, for he hadn't had any for months. It tasted so good!

The yearling was still the same coal black as the day he was born. He was practically all filled out and much more mature for his age, perhaps because of what he had been forced to go through at such an early age. Spring gave the world a whole new look and he was grateful that he had been given back the warmth, the birds, the grass, and everything else that the beautiful weather had to offer.

~~~~~

He came upon an old, abandoned ghost town some time in the next week or so. Not a single human being had been there for many, many years. As he wandered the old dirt roads, he knew that it was something that had been made by man and not by nature; but he also knew that there was nothing to fear since there was no sign of human activity at all.

He saw a three-story house which was crumbled quite badly in front and, curious to see what was inside, he approached the structure slowly, all his senses alert for any sign of danger. He reached the dilapidated outer brick wall and peered inside. A frightened mouse ran along the wooden floor and slid sideways through a door opening, disappearing into the dark room beyond it. The old furniture and other items in the room were covered with thick dust and grit and he could smell an unpleasant odor within the walls.

Withdrawing his head from the opening, he turned and looked at the remains of the old town. Suddenly becoming very much aware that he no longer wished to explore it, he carefully stepped back over the fallen rubble of the home and into the street. After glancing in the direction from which he had entered the town, he cantered off in the opposite direction and out of the area.

~~~~~

The next morning was simply beautiful. The new leaves on the trees were about the size of large cocoons and were very light green in color. The morning was warm and the yearling felt wonderfully alive.

That particular morning, because he felt so fresh and alive and full of energy, he decided to wander a bit and perhaps look for a new place in which to settle since he had been in the same location for almost a week. He wound his way through the beautiful thickness of the Oklahoma woods. The trees sent out their light, new fragrances and it made the yearling feel even better. He walked for quite some time before he came off the path, out of the woods, and into a very large clearing. The sight that was in front of him all but knocked him off his feet. For a while he could not move, but just stood there, staring. There they were, grazing, him being apparently unseen by them. His band, his beloved mother, and all of his colt-hood friends; there they were, he was sure of it!

The band was much larger than when he had lost them, and they still had the same wise leader. Standing at the edge of the woods, he was still unnoticed by them. He came out of his shock and took off toward them. The first horse to notice him was a bay mare. She let out a disturbed whinny, which made all the other horses look up, but not in his direction at first.

His mother saw him and they raced toward each other joyfully. When they reached each other, they sniffed, gave happy, playful nips to one another, and rolled on the ground, blowing and whinnying. Then the yearling's mother went to all the horses in the band with the yearling beside her, almost as if introducing him to them. When everyone had settled down, they went back to grazing as if the young horse had never left at all.

~~~~~~~

They were in rough country, a very rugged part of Oklahoma. The yearling liked that type of country; there was so much to explore and do.

One misty morning, as the band was grazing on the new spring grass, they heard some coyotes far, far off in the distance. It did not frighten them since they were still so far away. They wandered a bit while grazing and soon came to a steep ravine, about thirty feet away. Two of the young fillies got into a nippy fight over something or other and, without knowing how close they really were, went toppling over the edge. They landed on the soft grass at the bottom, stunned, but unhurt. A few of the other horses went to the edge and looked down. One of the fillies that had fallen into the ravine was lifting herself up, nothing hurt except her pride.

None of them knew exactly what to do. The stallion

assessed the situation and started down the steep side of the ravine; he was a sure-footed creature, about four years of age, and more experienced than he had been when the yearling had been lost. He was about halfway down when his right front hoof struck a loose rock. He skidded down the rest of the way, apparently unhurt. He picked himself up and checked the fillies over quickly. He almost seemed to be talking to them, asking them if they were all right and if they thought they would be able to make it back up.

Several of the horses at the top watched with dull interest. They didn't really care what happened below them, as long as they stayed safely at the top. The lead mare was concerned about them, however, especially the stallion, without whom she would have little help with providing the band protection. The horses below began nibbling at the sweet grass at the bottom of the ravine and most of those at the top also went back to grazing.

The yearling looked around him. Two of his buddies from his colt-hood were still there; they had been among those that had gone into the rocks and seen the owl with him when they were small. He did not know what had happened to several others he had known. Mountain lions, perhaps. Numerous mares were in the band now; many more than when the yearling had been separated from them. There were several new sucklings that spring, including his own mother's new filly. They were all of good quality; the stallion produced fine offspring. The majority of them were little fillies.

He turned his attention back to the horses at the bottom of the ravine. They were trying to get up the side of it, making several attempts at once, and then stopping to rest before trying again. They would get a few feet up before their hooves would scrape helplessly against the dry, clay side, and fall again. Their attempts were futile; the three of them were trapped down there.

The days passed and the bodies of the three horses at the

bottom of the ravine could be clearly seen. The lead mare was ready to move on and she gathered everyone together before leading them out of the area. It was late morning when they started out and they traveled a good distance, moving almost non-stop until dusk. They had come to a group of trees with a thick canopy when she called for them to stop. Most of the horses gathered under the trees to escape the steady drizzle of rain which had begun earlier in the afternoon. The yearling's two old friends, who seemed to prefer his company, grazed with him until the sun set and they all settled down to rest for the night.

~~~~~

The following days were quiet and they returned to a peaceful routine. The yearling now stood nearly fourteen hands. His legs were long and very powerful. He continued to mature at a fast rate and was very well proportioned. He showed such great spirit when he walked, it was more like a prance. He was a happy young horse.

The days passed quickly for the young horse and the rest of the band. The weather was warm and the gentle breezes brought many lovely scents to their delicate noses. One evening, as the sun was setting low, the leader did a very strange thing for no apparent reason at all. She moved the horses away from their site. They ran full speed, their leader in front and the black mustang pushing them forward from behind. They ran for some time before the leader signaled them to stop and they started grazing again. That was the end of that. They had stopped in a small clearing surrounded on three sides by thick woodland that would be ideal for shade when the daytime heat became too intense.

One night, the horses were disturbed by a small mountain lion lurking around not far away. Before they knew it, it was among them! One of the mares, who had been standing in the woods nearby, let out a shrill whinny, reared up, and struck her head on the massive branch of a tree. The powerful force of the blow killed her immediately and she crumpled to the ground.

Her colt, who had not been with her at the time, found her some time later and began to squeal in distress. A mare who heard his cries went to investigate and found the traumatized colt beside his mother. She observed the dead mare lying on the ground, and while she didn't know what had happened to her, she knew that she needed to get the trembling colt away from her. After several attempts, she was able to convince him to follow her out of the woods. She led him back to the rest of the horses and searched for a mare who she knew had recently lost her foal. She found her standing by herself and delivered the small colt to her care, satisfied that he would be all right.

The mountain lion had injured a couple of mares and their foals, but the horses, far outnumbering the cat, had been able to stop its attempts to harm them and it had retreated without doing much damage.

They moved on later that night, traveling south, and stopped on a hillside with a small spring and a few shade trees. Although they did not know it, they were getting closer to civilization.

Two days later, they were grazing on the hillside. The yearling and one of his closest friends were standing a short distance away from the rest of the band. The sun was shining and the air was perfectly still as they nibbled on the thick, green grass.

Not one of them saw the man and the horse appear just over the top of the hill and come to an abrupt stop. His horse stood perfectly still as the man scanned the horses in front of them and reached for his rope. He seemed to have his focus on the two horses standing off to the side of the large group. The yearling suddenly sensed something amiss and raised his head. He did not see the expertly thrown rope until it fell neatly over head and onto his shoulders, and by that time it was too late.

Feeling the pressure of the rope just above his shoulders, he was stunned and looked toward the man and the horse, who were coming toward him, the man looping and securing the extra rope in front of him as they neared. The rider was in complete control of his mount, an impossibly calm dapple gray gelding. The horse and the man had obviously done this before and they worked very well together. The man spoke quietly to his horse and it, in turn, seemed to try to calm the black yearling. Nickering softly, the gelding appeared to be trying to convince the yearling to cooperate.

The other end of the rope around the yearling's neck was securely attached to a thick metal ring which was crafted into the big gelding's saddle. The yearling struggled at first, planting his front feet on the ground and pulling against the rope, ears pinned. The big gelding braced and dutifully counteracted the yearling's attempts while the man continued to talk to him.

The yearling was pretty sure that the rest of the band had fled the area in fear; he couldn't really blame them. The only sounds he heard were coming from the man and the gelding, and he tried not to think of the lonely time that he had spent separated from his friends. Trying not to panic, he stopped pulling on the rope long enough to quickly look around.

It was just the three of them on the side of the hill. He took a deep breath and snorted at the gelding.

The gelding whinnied softly and all three were motionless for a moment, the two horses looking at each other. The yearling made no other attempt to struggle and the man waited, apparently hoping the black horse would relax.

The bright afternoon air remained completely calm and

the two horses' breathing gradually slowed. When the man was fairly confident that the yearling would follow the gelding's lead, he slowly turned his horse toward the top of the hill in the direction from which they had come. The yearling pawed the ground and took a quick step forward. The man nudged his horse and they began to move, climbing the hill. The yearling lowered his head and soundlessly followed the gray horse.

~~~~~

They walked for a very long time. The gentle disposition of the gelding and the non-threatening manner of the man allowed the yearling to accept the situation and after some time he even quickened his pace to walk just behind and to the side of them. The gelding would occasionally turn his head and nicker softly to him.

Finally, they came to two large pick-up trucks parked on a wide dirt path. One of the trucks had a trailer hitched to the back of it. There was a man accompanied by a young woman sitting on the open tailgate of one of the trucks and they turned to watch the trio approach.

The man on the gray gelding dismounted, spoke to his horse, and walked over to the couple. The three of them had a discussion before the two men began to walk back to the gelding and the yearling. The young woman went to the back of the trailer, opened the door, and set up a ramp.

The yearling was tired and still relatively calm. He wanted to stay close to his new friend and when the men began to lead the gelding toward the trailer, the yearling followed tentatively. It didn't take the men long to get both horses into the trailer and ready to travel.

When the door closed behind them, the yearling looked to the gelding for reassurance. The big gelding remained calm and this comforted the yearling. He was very tired but he couldn't help being curious about where he was and where they were going. He looked around the trailer as it began to move and steadied himself on his feet as his companion whinnied softly to him.

The trailer jarred the two horses quite a bit. The truck traveled slowly and the ride was very long. The yearling was exhausted and leaned against the wall much of the time. They went through fields, over hills, and even through a fairly large creek. The trailer bumped and jolted for more than an hour before they finally came to a dirt road that was much smoother than the terrain on which they had already traveled. It was a relief to both of the horses and they were finally able to relax for the remainder of the trip.

~~~~~

The truck finally stopped and a few minutes later the door of the trailer swung open. The bright light hurt the yearling's eyes at first and he flinched and blinked several times to adjust to the light.

The gelding was unloaded first and the yearling felt the rope gently tugging at his neck. He managed to get himself down the ramp to join his friend and was unexpectedly disappointed to see that the man who had roped him was no longer with the couple. They had stopped in front of a large, gray building and he didn't like the looks of it at all.

The rope still connected the two horses and the yearling followed as the woman led the gelding into the building. The man walked with them and kept his hand on the rope close to the yearling's neck. Once inside, the man guided him into a stall, closed the door and then removed the other end of the rope from the gelding's saddle. He wound the rope, hung it up just outside the door, and walked away.

The yearling looked around the stall. It was tiny and dirty straw covered the floor. There was water in a dirty bucket and a little bit of hay lying in the corner. That was it. With barely enough room to move around, he lowered his head and curiously smelled at the bucket, feeling the weight of the rope caught in his thick mane. He had never drank from a bucket but he was thirsty and took a long drink.

It wasn't long before he heard the loud voices of men.

"They leavin' today, Dennis?" one man asked.

The reply came loud and clear, "Yup, Bill's drivin' out to Denver for an auction. Supposed to be some real horse buyers there."

The two men talked while the yearling and the rest of the horses in the building were loaded onto a large truck. The interior of the truck contained partitions and the experienced handlers managed to get each horse into one of the small, separate compartments. The yearling looked for the gray gelding among the horses and didn't see him.

They rode for a long time. While it was clear that some of the horses were very stressed, the yearling tried hard to stay calm. He wanted to know where they were going. Finally, the truck stopped, only to start moving again after a few minutes; they had only stopped for gas.

The ride went on and on; it seemed never-ending. There were no windows at all for the horses to look out of or get any fresh air and it began to smell. The driver couldn't make turns at all and had it not been for the little stalls, the horses surely would have fallen.

At last the truck stopped, and this time the doors were flung open. The horses jumped and blinked their eyes. They were unloaded and led into a very large room with rails all around it and a large doorway in the corner. Behind the rails, the room was full of people.

He heard a loud voice that seemed to be coming from nowhere. "Start the bidding, please..."

There was a small voice from somewhere.

"Three hundred. Do I hear three-fifty?" the voice boomed.

Again, he heard a distant voice.

"Three fifty over there in the blue shirt. Do I hear four hundred?"

Silence.

"Do I hear three seventy-five?"

A small voice came from somewhere.

"Do I hear three eighty?"

Silence.

"Three seventy-five going once, twice, three times! Sold to the man over there in the red shirt."

This went on and on and it was quite some time before the yearling could see that the horses in the room with him were being led outside through the big doorway in the corner, one by one.

Soon, the men came to him, shoved a too-small halter on his head after some difficulty, and pulled him in front of all the people. Hundreds of people that stood before him let out hundreds of gasps. It was true that he was handsome. Cigarette smoke drifted to him and he was petrified.

"Start the bidding, please ..."

He just stood there, in a daze, shocked.

"... four hundred seventy-five in the corner ..."

He stared straight ahead.

"Sold to the man in the back for five hundred dollars!" the voice boomed.

He was led, half fighting, into a one-horse trailer and he made himself stand still while the door was closed tightly behind him. It smelled good inside. There was a small window at his side where light filtered in. Voices floated in from outside.

"Sure got a nice one, Mel."

"Yeah, well, I don't even know why I bought him. Don't even need any more horses on the ranch. I should have listened to Lucy and not even come today. I can't even come to an auction without buyin' *something*," the man called Mel replied.

The first man spoke again. "Well, good luck with him."

The two men shook hands and Mel got into the truck and they started off.

~~~~~~

As the trailer bounced along the uneven road, the yearling was not aware that he was getting farther and farther away from what had once been home to him. The jolts came inconsistently and forcefully. His head came so close to the ceiling a few times that he began to crouch down whenever he felt the truck beginning to lurch. Fortunately, the ride was not too long and they stopped in about a half hour.

He was carefully unloaded by Mel and two stable hands. They led him to a large stall with fresh, sweet straw, water and hay. They then shut the half-door and went back outside to let the young horse get used to his new home. They sat on the concrete steps and talked.

"I sure hope Lucy don't mind. I think she'll understand why I bought him. After all, Paula's been wanting her own horse for about as long as I can remember," Mel said.

One of the stable hands, Johnny, replied, "Wish ya all the luck in the world, Boss, but we both know how the missus is."

The other boy, Nat, said, "Aw, we all know she'll love him. Besides, she loves Paula just as much as you do. She'll be happy you got her a horse."

The men went on talking until they heard Lucy Ramble's small pick-up truck coming up the gravel driveway. She was bringing Paula home from school.

29

"Get ready, Boss," Johnny said. "Here she comes."

Lucy and Paula walked up to the men slowly; obviously something was wrong. When they got there, Lucy talked with the three men. Paula said nothing. Pretty soon her father wanted to know what was wrong.

"Paula," he said. "What's bothering you? Did something happen at school today?"

Paula blinked back tears, went over to her father and sat down. "My whole class, *everyone*, has their own horse," she began, "except me. Everyone is going riding this weekend, camping out on Saturday night and everything – *if* you have your own horse!" At this point, she buried her head on Mel's shoulder and began to cry.

A smile came over Mel's face.

Lucy saw it and became angry. "Now, Mel, I do not find it the least bit funny! Think about when you were thirteen," she protested.

Paula lifted her head and looked at her father in disbelief. He had never done this to her before, laughed at her like this. She was about to get up and run to the house when Mel spoke.

"You see, Lucy, you have it all wrong." He looked at his daughter. "Paula, I think it would be a good idea for you to go muck out Army's old stall. I don't think it's been cleaned since he left."

~~~~~~

Paula, confused by what her father had said about her mom being wrong, got up slowly, half in a daze because of her father's actions, and went into the big barn. The stall that she needed to clean was located at the far end. Army's owner had boarded him at the barn until about a week before, and his stall had been empty ever since.

After she went in, Mel, Johnny and Nat sat there with funny looks of expectation on their faces. Lucy just wanted to know what was going on and, at this point, was not very happy with her husband at all.

Paula picked up a stick from the floor of the barn as she entered. She slid it along the wall as she walked down the aisle with empty stalls on either side of her; the horses were pastured during the day and wouldn't return until that evening. She stopped about halfway to the stall she was going to and entered a large room with all sorts of tack, shovels, and pitchforks, among other things. She picked up a nice, new pitchfork and put it in an old blue wheelbarrow. Then she wheeled it out the door and shut it behind her. As she got closer to her destination, the smell of fresh straw reached her nose. She stopped in another room, loaded a bale of straw onto the wheelbarrow and went out into the aisle again.

When she reached the stall, her head was still hung low as she thought about the camping trip that everyone else in her class would be taking. Then she heard it. It scared her out of her wits. It was very faint but she was totally unprepared for it – the nicker of a horse. She looked up, startled, and through the half door, on a brand new layer of sweet straw, lay the most beautiful horse she ever saw in her entire life.

At once, the whole picture came to her, the grins of her father and Johnny and Nat, and the unusual statement that her father had made about her mom being wrong. Instantly, she knew that he was hers!

She gave a shriek of joy and went tearing down the aisle back to her parents. Then, she changed her mind and decided to pet the horse first. Then, because she knew that wouldn't be right, she turned and ran down the aisle again and out the door.

"Oh, Dad, he's simply gorgeous! Thank you so much! I love you!" she cried.

"Wait a minute, now, Paula. This doesn't mean that you can go on that camping trip. He's a wild mustang and can't even be led right yet. We'll need to leave him alone for a while and let him get used to his new surroundings before we start anything. It's a process, Paula, you know that," Mel said, smiling.

"Who cares? I got my own horse! He'll get the best care and attention out of all the horses on the ranch because he's mine and I'll be givin' it to him! Oh, thank you so much, mom, dad. Thank you!"

That evening after supper, Paula went straight to the barn. It was always so peaceful and she loved to be there, especially when something was wrong or bothering her. Now it would be even better because she had a horse there, too!

Since it was getting dark, she put on the new lights that had just been installed in the barn and ran down the aisle until she came to Army's old stall. The black horse was lying peacefully on the straw with his legs curled under him. She stood there silently for a few moments just looking at him. Quietly, she began to talk to him as she thought about her plans.

First, he'll need a name, she thought, and I'm not going to name him Midnight or Blackie or anything as plain as that. Looking at him, she could see tiny amounts of dust from the fresh straw that had settled on his coat, vividly contrasting with his pitch black color.

"You're a little dusty, there, sweetie," she giggled. At that moment, she was reminded of a kid named Dusty who she'd had a terrible crush on way back in kindergarten and made her decision. She would call her new horse Dusty.

"I hope you like the name I gave you, Dusty," she cooed to the resting horse. "Do you like your new stall? I hope so, but we're gonna have to get you out of there soon so you can meet the other horses and get some exercise. I'll start working on you as soon as Daddy says it's okay. Will you be good for me? Please? Well, it's gettin' dark, so I better go in now so mom and dad don't get worried about me. You sleep tight and be good."

She finished her speech and started down the aisle, stopping at every stall, saying 'good night' to each of the horses and making sure all the doors were securely closed. She turned off the lights as she went out the door and started down the small hill toward the house.

~~~~~~

In the days that followed, Paula's happiness shrank slightly; the black mustang sure was a problem. He would not let Paula or her parents even get close enough with the halter to try to get it on him.

Dusty knew that Paula was not going to hurt him. He had slowly grown attached to the girl, waiting for her visits each day after school and feeling a sense of sadness after she left. Tonight, he lay on the straw, which was getting a bit dirty, though it really didn't bother him, and had the first good night's sleep that he'd had since he was taken away from the band.

It was raining the next day and Paula didn't come for a long, long time. Dusty was beginning to get worried and was afraid she would never get there. Just when he was about to give up, the lights switched on and Paula came down the aisle. She was wearing a shiny thing around her body and a smaller one on her head. *Sometimes these creatures are very strange.* She had something red and shiny in her hand and she held it out to Dusty. His first thought was to go over and see what it was, but instinct overcame him. He backed up a little. Paula held it out further, to no avail.

33

Paula spoke quietly, "Dad was right. It's too soon." She dropped the thing on the ground beside Dusty and it landed with a soft thud. She talked to him for a few minutes more and then left, leaving him alone. He took a slow step toward the thing, slightly afraid. He put his nose toward it, touched it softly, and jumped back. It was cold, but it had smelled good, like nothing he had ever smelled before! He approached it again with extreme care. He extended his long neck and touched it again. This time he was prepared and did not jump back when he felt its coldness. It smelled so good. He lipped it, as he had done with his first hay and oats given to him. He took a tiny chunk out of it and chewed slowly, half expecting the thing to bite him back.

It was delicious! He savored the thing, eating it slowly, as if to make it last longer. This was his first experience with an apple.

~~~~~

Paula's work at school began to suffer. During classes, she would think about nothing but Dusty – how she would go about breaking him, how she would ride him, what things she would teach him, and things of that sort. She managed to keep her grades to a high C, but she knew her parents' thoughts. They knew that she was an extremely bright student and expected her to get all A's and B's. If these grades that she had been getting recently on classwork and tests made a big impression on her report card, she would have something other than Dusty to worry about.

She hadn't told anyone at school about Dusty, not because she was ashamed of him, but because she wanted to surprise everyone on the next class ride. She didn't know if she could keep it from her best friend, Sue, long enough, though. Sue had noticed her strange behavior lately and had

34

asked Paula if there was anything wrong. Still, Paula had kept it to herself, though, inside, she had wanted to tell Sue so badly. She simply had to keep it to herself until the next class ride at the end of the school year. Her father had finally given his approval to begin working with Dusty the following Saturday.

The week went by all too slow for Paula. When the bell finally rang on Friday, Paula went racing out the door without a word to anyone. She hoped her friends wouldn't be mad at her; they would understand. It seemed like it took three hours for her mother to get there to take her home, but nothing could spoil her high spirits now. When she got in the truck, she was all smiles and humming a little song to herself.

Lucy started the conversation, "Well, Paula, this sure is a big change from the little girl I knew this past week." Paula hated it when her mother called her a "little girl". After all, she was thirteen years old. Anyway, she was too happy to be bothered by things like that now.

"Drive faster, mom. I want to get home and start on Dusty," she pleaded.

"Oh, was that what it was? You couldn't hold out all week to start on Dusty? Well, let me tell you something, Paula. A horse is not something that you can rush things with. Your father paid five hundred dollars for that horse of yours, and that's an awful lot of money for a horse with unknown parentage. So, if I were you, and didn't want to ruin him or make an enemy out of my father, I would take my time with him. Now, if that sounded like a lecture, I'm sorry, because it wasn't meant to sound that way." Lucy was gentle, but firm.

"I know, mom. I remember what happened when Daddy tried to rush things with Bomber; all those dealers angry with him and all. Don't worry, I'll take my time and do the best I can with him," Paula replied, deep in thought.

"That's good, Paula," Lucy began, "because your father

and I both know what you are capable of doing with a horse. We saw that with Sherry." Paula recalled the first pony she had ever trained by herself – a tiny buckskin Shetland. Here, the conversation stopped as the truck sped along the country road toward home.

~~~~~

Lucy Ramble's little blue pickup truck crept slowly up the gravel driveway. Before it even had a chance to stop, Paula was out of it and racing for the house. Once inside, she slammed her books down on the kitchen table and, without even stopping to have her usual after-school snack, headed straight for the barn. Partway there, she remembered that she had forgotten Dusty's apple and started back toward the house. When she got inside, her mother was there, starting supper.

"Now, Paula, don't forget what I told you on the way home ... if you try to rush, you'll just make things worse, and maybe even ruin ---" she began. But Paula cut her off before she could finish.

"I know, I know, Mom! How many times are you going to tell me that? You even said that you and dad could trust me after you saw what I did with Sherry." At the mention of that name, Paula's mouth turned from a frustrated smile to a slight frown of sadness, and she looked away.

Her mother saw this and said, "I just don't want anything to happen that could hurt you."

Paula replied, "Well, you're hurting me more than you think by not trusting me."

"Oh, Paula, it's not that I don't trust you ... well, you just go out there and do the best you can and I'll be more than happy," Lucy replied.

With that, Paula's face brightened and she ran out the

door. Then, realizing that she'd forgotten Dusty's apple again, came running back in. She went directly to the refrigerator and picked out the nicest apple she could find, went over to the sink, washed it off and headed outside once more.

Dusty was lying peacefully on his straw when Paula got there. She could tell that he had been dozing.

"Oh, you beautiful, beautiful thing, you," she whispered softly to him. "Now, for days you have been lying here doing nothing but getting fat and lazy, even in that dirty old straw. Well, it's time for you to get out, and behave," she said this last part with soft authority and sternness.

Dusty had come to look forward to Paula's daily visits and especially the delicious red things she brought along with her. But when he saw Paula starting to open the stall door very slowly, he forgot all the nice things about her and a look of fear came into his eyes.

"Now, Dusty," Paula whispered softly and soothingly, "don't be like that. I don't want to hurt you. No, not at all. That would be the last thing in the world I would want to do to you." She spoke very quietly, slurring many of her words, and just as she had hoped and expected, it calmed him down. The fear went out of his eyes and she could see him becoming more relaxed. Then, still talking quietly to him, Paula opened the door a crack, not showing her fear. She opened it wider and entered slowly, not closing the door behind her in case of an emergency.

To Paula's surprise, Dusty did not move a muscle, but stood there, eyeing her, with absolutely no fear in his eyes at all. The next thing she knew, everything went black.

~~~~~~

"That horse has got to go!" Mel Ramble's voice rang out, "I don't care what I paid for it or anything else for that matter. It's got to go!"

Lucy's voice was calmer and quieter, yet firm, "Mel, she has gotten so attached to him and if you took him away from her now, especially after *you* got him for her, it would just crush her."

Mel spoke. "She's already crushed." His voice was sarcastic, yet serious. "Lucy, he is going and that's all there is to it. For a horse to come crashing down on some poor, helpless little girl is too much and is not fit for anyone to have. I'm taking him to the glue factory first thing tomorrow morning. And Lucy, nothin's gonna stop me!"

Lucy's voice was still calm, "Mel, you said yourself that's not how it happened. You didn't give the girl a chance. Don't you think she even deserves that? That horse means so much to her and you'll just be hurting her worse if you take him away from her now."

"One could even say it was your fault, Lucy," Mel's voice was getting louder and angrier. "After all, you're the one that let her go out and try to work with a horse that has hardly seen a human being in its life, most likely. You know you should have let me at least green break and teach it the basics for Paula, then she could have taken it from there."

At this, Lucy couldn't stand it any longer and ran outside to the truck, tears coming to her eyes. She headed straight for the hospital, driving almost blindly. Almost an hour later, she pulled into the parking lot of the hospital where Paula was being treated. She walked into the lobby and gave some information at the desk, where she was told to go to room 375.

When she reached the closed door, she heard a TV and some giggling coming from inside the room. Slowly, she knocked on the door.

"Who is it?" called a voice from inside. It was Paula.

"Mommy," Lucy replied, her voice a bit shaky from what she had to tell her daughter.

"Oh!" called the excited voice, "Come in!"

Lucy entered the room, still half in a daze. Then, realizing Paula would notice something was wrong, she snapped herself out of it and went over and sat down on the edge of the bed. She spoke, trying her hardest to sound natural, "How do you feel, honey?"

Paula replied, her voice happy, "Oh, just fine, but, would you mind telling me what happened?"

"Well, Paula," Lucy began slowly, "no one was there except you so we don't really know, but your daddy took a look after the ambulance left. From what he saw, he said that he doesn't think that Dusty himself hit you. He thinks he reared up and knocked that loose beam that Al was supposed to fix on top of you, because it was lying a couple feet from where you were."

"Well, I must have a tender head or something," Paula said, but added quickly, "It's nothing to worry about, now I just have a little bit of a headache. I can't wait to get home and start on Dusty again, he deserves another chance, you know?" Here, she smiled.

"That's what I have to talk to you about, Paula," Lucy began weakly. "I know that he deserves another chance, but your father doesn't. He's taking Dusty away tomorrow." She tried to make it short.

Paula's face looked as though she had just seen a ghost. At first she couldn't say a word but then began, "That's not fair." She wouldn't cry. "Dusty is a wonderful horse, he just needs another chance. I was probably one of the first people he ever saw besides his shippers."

Though she tried, she couldn't keep the tears from coming. Paula never saw Dusty again.

~~~~~

Mel was leading Magic, the old ponying horse, out of her stall. He needed her help try to lead Dusty to the trailer. He led her up to Dusty's stall, where he stopped. Dusty was standing in the corner, and seemed to be looking nowhere. Mel began cursing at him and telling him it was all his fault for what had happened to Paula. Finally, he stopped and opened the stall door, a little nervous about what had to be done.

Dusty eyed him curiously, unafraid, just as he had done with Paula.

"Don't you dare try anything, horse. You ain't that much bigger than me, you know," Mel spoke threateningly.

Surprisingly, Dusty allowed the halter to be put on him, after some fighting of course, but it did go on. Mel then pulled him over to Magic, who had been standing there quietly the whole time, and led them out of the barn. Then he hopped onto Magic bareback and started for the same truck that had brought Dusty there. He had no trouble getting to the truck because Dusty followed Magic quietly, but getting him into the trailer was a different story. He wouldn't walk up the ramp and Mel couldn't force him up no matter how hard he tried. After several attempts, he tied the two horses onto an old hitching post and ran to the barn to get some feed.

That worked. Dusty walked right up the ramp after Mel had placed the feed in the front of the trailer. He put Magic away, got into the truck, and pulled out of the driveway.

~~~~~~

Mel knew where he could take the horse and be guaranteed that no kid in the country would ever be exposed to it again. It was a shady operation and although he'd never been there, he knew exactly where it was located.

When he arrived, he saw a throng of people and some miserable-looking horses scattered around a run-down barn. He parked the truck, got out and unloaded Dusty with little trouble. The man who seemed to be in charge was discussing the future of an old gray mare with a man and a woman. Mel secured Dusty to the trailer, leaned against the truck, and waited his turn.

It wasn't long before a man dressed in casual clothes approached and, without saying a word, began examining Dusty. After a few moments, he spoke, "You're not giving this beautiful horse to this crazy outfit, are you?" he asked in disbelief.

"He's a killer," Mel replied flatly.

"I'll buy him from you." The man's eyes were getting bigger.

"I told you, he's a killer and he's not fit for anyone in his right mind to have." Mel was getting impatient.

"Well, then, I'm not in my right mind. I'll give ya six hundred for him," the man pressed on. "That's a lot more than you'll get for him here."

Mel needed the money and the way he thought, he would be out a killer. "I'll take it," he replied. "When can I have my money?"

"Ah, I knew you looked like a man with sense," the stranger looked overwhelmed. "Right now, you can have your money right now, of course." He removed an overstuffed billfold from his pocket, pulled out six hundred dollar bills, handed them carelessly to Mel and untied the lead rope. He then led Dusty, without another word to Mel, to a nice two-horse trailer.

Mel mumbled as he opened the door of the truck, "Looks like you're gettin' more than ya deserve, horse." Then, he looked at the money in his hand and a smile spread over his face.

Dusty took to the man immediately; there was just something about him that he liked. He let the man load him into the trailer with no trouble. There was another horse already inside, a sorrel mare. The truck started moving with an unintentional jolt and they rode for what seemed like a long time to Dusty until they finally stopped. The ride had not been too tiring since the man was a very skillful driver and rounded turns very well, which, if not done correctly, can be exhausting. A couple minutes after the truck stopped, the doors were opened and the bright sunlight shined into the trailer, giving Dusty a wonderful feeling inside. The man carefully unloaded him and Dusty looked around.

There was a large, white house with three balconies and a big green lawn. To the side were a couple of beautiful, elegant outbuildings, also white. Beyond the house was a wooded area, in front of which stood an extravagant red barn with a covered paddock.

The man led Dusty into the paddock, removed the lead rope from the halter and softly patted his shoulder. "You just relax, big guy," he said. "I can't stay right now, but I'll be back a little later to see how you're doing." He went out the gate and walked toward the house.

~~~~~

His first night there was both good and bad at the same time. It was good because the stall that he was led into was filled with a thick layer of clean, dry, aromatic straw. There was a large window near the top of the high ceiling, so he couldn't break it, and he was given the first bran mash he'd ever had. It was simply delicious, and if he could have filled himself up on it until he burst, he would have. He loved this new place and everything about it.

The bad thing was not serious, something that almost every living creature experiences from time to time - he felt somewhat anxious in his new surroundings and almost homesick. He kept thinking about Paula and had trouble sleeping the first night.

The man who had purchased him was Gene Summers, an outstanding breeder and trainer of all types of horses. He lived with his wife, Julie, and two sons and a daughter. The oldest son was Jeremy, who was fifteen years old. Next came John, who was twelve, and then Maureen, who was eleven years old. They were a happy family; very well knit together with a strong love and passion for one another. The children rarely fought, though they were not exactly what one might call perfect angels. They all went to the same school, which was for all grades, and the whole family spent most of their free time with the horses, training them for shows, which were usually held at Three Oaks Race Track.

They had many types of horses, including Morgans, Thoroughbreds, Appaloosas, hunters, Arabians, and, like Dusty, mustangs. They had excellent facilities, and three extremely large barns, which, all together, sheltered approximately 150 head. The first week that he was there, Dusty thought that life was just going to mean not having to do any work or anything of the sort; but after the first week, things changed.

He was standing in his stall one morning, feeling a little restless, when Gene came into the barn, whistling. He had a halter in his hand. There were about forty other horses in the barn with Dusty; it was packed almost full. Gene, on his way to Dusty's stall, talked to and patted each horse gently. He was very sensitive to the horses. His belief was that horses were just like people, therefore, they should be treated like people. He respected each one as an individual.

He finally got to Dusty's stall, and, without fear or hesitation, opened the door. Dusty's eyes widened. He had begun to trust men, but not as far as letting them come into the same stall that he was in! He backed up and snorted. Gene made no move whatsoever to get out of the stall. Dusty was becoming more frightened and pressed up against the padded wall. Gene came closer. Dusty's fear turned to anger and he began to rear up to strike with his forelegs.

Suddenly, he remembered what he had done to the little girl that he had almost actually loved. He remembered knocking the loose beam down and saw the pained expression on the girl's face as it came crashing down upon her head. He lowered his body, not striking Gene.

"Had a change of heart, did you?" Gene said slowly, softly. Sure that Dusty would not even think to act up again, he put the halter over his shoulder and walked the few necessary steps to reach the horse. Dusty just stood there, his eyes wide and nostrils flared. Gene raised his hand very slowly, not wanting to scare or upset him any more than he already was. Dusty allowed him to do that, but when it came to touching him, that was something else altogether. The second Gene laid his fingers on Dusty's forehead, he panicked. He turned two complete circles, almost knocking Gene off his feet, and quickly got over to the other side of the large stall, hopping and twisting. He was making quite a bit of noise and it sent almost every other horse in the barn into a commotion.

By this time, Gene was a little shaken up and very discouraged with the horse since its behavior up to that point had been remarkably good. Trying to control his temper, he exited the stall, slamming the door behind him, and went to calm down the other horses.

~~~~~~

44

After Gene left, Dusty stood there resting. He was confused. He hadn't meant to misbehave. He thought about being in the fields and the mountains and what his life had been like not so long ago. He thought of his old friends and the fun that they had had; but he also thought of Paula and the people here who had been so nice to him. He didn't want to make trouble. He hoped to be able to show that to Gene and do better when he returned.

Gene came into the barn every morning as usual, but instead of talking to Dusty like all the rest of the horses, he would silently feed him and ignore him completely. Dusty wasn't sure what this meant, but he knew it wasn't good. He got very upset about it and one day Gene noticed this.

"Had enough of my treatment, did you?" He spoke softly, as if all was forgiven, which it was. "I give that to all my horses that act like you did. Works every time." He patted Dusty.

Dusty was very sorry about what he had done. He wasn't stupid and he knew that he had caused his kind new master a great deal of difficulty and sorrow. Even though he was as sorry as he was, he could never tell his master, but he could show him.

When Gene came in to feed around dusk that night, Dusty was as quiet as he could be. He didn't try to nip Gene's hand as he put the bucket in, or even kick the padded sides of his stall to make those funny sounds that he liked. He was very good. Gene noticed this and spoke to him, "Are you feeling better now, old boy?" Gene's voice was soft and soothing. "We all have our bad days, I won't hold it none against ya. You're a good kid, you just have a little to learn is all. Be good next time and don't cause such a riot, okay?" Gene left Dusty's stall and went on feeding, whistling as he worked.

That evening, as the family was having their evening meal, the conversation directed itself to the horses.

"Well, the black one's shapin' up," began Gene, "I think he looks forward to my visits like the rest of 'em do now. And he even lets me reach over the door to pet him. I got good intentions for him later on, after he's trained real good."

Maureen spoke, "He's real nice, daddy. I like him. To bad he don't ---"

Julie interrupted Maureen here, "Doesn't!"

"I'm sorry – doesn't! Too bad he don't --- doesn't," she corrected herself again, "have a name," she finished.

John spoke, "Girls! Always worried about dumb things like names and curtains and dolls... all the dumb things! Why not worry about the training for the beast or something like that?"

Maureen was furious. "He's not a beast, and things like that are not dumb!"

Gene stopped the argument at this point. "That's enough, kids. Now Maureen, since you're so interested in names, why don't we let you have the honor of naming him? What do you say?"

"Oh, thank you, Daddy! Do I get to pick any name at all? Do you know if he had a name before you got him?" She was so excited.

"Now, wait a minute, Maureen," Gene was laughing. "One thing at a time. Yes, you may pick any name at all. No, I don't know if he had a name before I got him. Fathers just don't think about important stuff like that." He winked at John, who gave him a grin in return.

Maureen began thinking of a name aloud until she was told by her mom not to worry about it until after she was done eating. After that, all conversation stopped and Maureen ate quickly, wondering to herself what would be a good name to pin on Dusty.

After supper, she went directly to her bedroom. She

wanted to think of a special name for the black horse and she thought that going through some of her horse books might give her some ideas. She wanted a good, interesting name, perhaps something Indian, like Apache or Cheyenne. But after thinking about it for a while, she decided that Indian names were much too common.

She sat cross-legged on her bed, paging through her books. Through the partially open door, she could hear her brothers playing a board game in the next room. From what she could hear, it sounded like John was losing. She heard the dice hit the board and then an exuberant "Yeah! Snake eyes!" from John.

Immediately, she thought of the black horse's big dark eyes. To her, they always looked so serious and thoughtful.

Snake Eyes! That's a good name! I'll call him Snake for short!

And so her decision was made, although she would never tell John that he had had anything to do with it.

~~~~~

Snake was living like a king. His stall was always kept clean and on the occasional cool morning, he was given the hot bran mash that he loved! He was fed the highest quality oats and hay and his days were spent pastured with many other horses. Gene began to saddle and bridle the trail horses in plain view of the black horse, hoping that he would see that it caused them no harm and ease his anxiety. It wouldn't be long before his real training would begin.

Maureen went to see Snake every day. She always brought him something good, maybe an apple or a carrot or some sugar or a good, hot bran mash. He was treated with the best of care and had the finest facilities west of Norton.

One morning, Gene came into the barn with a halter and

47

lead rope. He had given Snake plenty of time to get accustomed to his surroundings and was ready to try again. Snake had not forgotten the day that he had caused such a great fuss in the barn. He had been quite embarrassed and did not intend to ever do such a thing again.

Gene approached Snake's stall holding the halter just in front of him and to his surprise the horse seemed very curious, showing no anxiety at all. Talking softly to him, Gene reached over the door and let him sniff the halter. He gently slid it along his neck and shoulder and allowed the horse to sniff at it again. The horse showed no obvious signs of fear and within a few minutes, the halter was on! He opened the door, led Snake out of the barn, and quietly walked him in the paddock. He was shocked at the drastic improvement in the horse; the animal seemed to want to please him and was very obedient. He continued this daily routine for a half hour each day and the horse's progress was impressive. He soon began longeing Snake daily and they worked very well together. Snake made nice, neat circles and always worked quietly. He was a good horse – very quick to learn. He used his head a lot, more than any other horse Gene had ever seen. Snake was definitely making him proud of the time and money he had invested in him.

One night the east barn was in a riot. Horses were kicking and screaming in their stalls, and some had even managed to escape. When Snake became aware of what was happening, he too, started kicking and screaming that spine-tingling stallion scream. He knew he must get out of the stall if he was to live. He knew this because this was not his first experience with fire; somehow, he must get out!

He was kicking with all his might, as were most of the other horses in the barn. Finally, the side of his stall started to give way. He could hear the boards groaning under the force of his kicks when suddenly his left hind leg smashed

clear through the wood all the way to his hock.
Hysterically, he pulled his leg forward, trying to free it from the wood's grip. The pain was horrible; with every effort he made to get his leg out, he did more damage to himself. Screaming and gasping for air, he collapsed onto his front legs.

It was then that Gene and Julie appeared. They were working together as quickly as they could to rescue the horses, opening stall doors and frantically trying to get them moving in the right direction.

"Let me get a halter on him!" Gene shouted to Julie over the noise. "He'll never stay on property!"

She grabbed the halter that was hanging just outside Snake's stall and tried desperately to get it onto his head while Gene went around behind him. He carefully lifted Snake's leg up and partially through the hole in the partition. Snake could feel enormous relief from the pain as soon as Gene did this and he was able to get it free of the wall completely. He stood with his full weight on all four legs, twisted his neck between Julie and the door, and bolted into the aisle. Julie could only stand there and watch him go, the halter still clutched in her fingers.

~~~~~

He ran about two miles before he finally stopped; he didn't want to take any chances on being caught again. He knew that people could be kind and he had been treated well by many of them, but he was wild and probably always would be. He walked a bit before he saw water, stopped for a cool drink, and started walking again. The terrain was completely flat with no trees and he continued on with only a very slight limp.

He walked another ten miles or so before he saw

anything different from the monotonous scenery that he'd already covered - a ranch ahead of him and to the right. Brian York and his wife and kids were the residents. They had close to 900 acres and about 170 head of steer and 20 quarter horses. The ranch consisted of a fairly large house, two large barns, two corrals and a pond on the west side of the property. Most of Brian's land was fenced, providing plenty of space for the steer and horses to graze, and since they got along very well, they were able to share the same pasture areas. Brian and Dave, his son, were out harvesting one of the hay fields when Snake arrived. It was late summer and the evening sun was finally starting to slide down in the sky.

Snake stood there, watching them, not knowing if he should go forward or change direction. He started to turn, but he was so thirsty and the York's pond was tantalizing. Finally, he started down a small crest toward the pond at a gallop. If he was going to get caught, at least he would get something to drink first.

He was almost to the pond, still unnoticed, when Dave suddenly cried, "Look, Dad, that's not one of ours, is it?"

Brian turned and looked, awed by the beauty and elegance of Snake. Finally, he replied, "No, Dave, that's no quarter horse, it can't be one of ours. Looks wild to me, one of the prettiest wild horses I've ever seen, except Bullet."

Bullet had been another wild horse that had wandered off the range onto Brian's place. At first, he'd been just a skinny little thing, but Brian and Dave had put weight on him and worked him into a handsome animal.

They began to approach him very slowly and he stood still and watched them, somehow knowing that he did not need to fear them. He lowered his head and took a long, cool drink as they continued to make their way toward him. After a moment, he raised his head and looked at them. He thought of his friends and wondered if he would ever be able to find them again, but he also wondered if these people might have some delicious treats for him somewhere, too.

Brian stopped walking, but Dave, who was staring at Snake, continued to move forward. He and the horse watched each other, and neither one was afraid.

Dave slowly reached out his hand to Snake as he approached him, talking gently to the horse. When his hand touched Snake, the horse flinched slightly, but Dave did not pull his hand away and the horse remained still, concentrating on the boy. Slowly, Dave began to slide his hand down Snake's neck as Brian walked up behind him.

"See that, Dad?" Dave began, "He's only *half* wild; someone's worked with him before."

Brian spoke, "David, you can't keep him. He's not yours."

Dave's hand went limp and fell to his side. He just *had* to have this horse!

"But Dad, we don't even know where he came from or how far he came before he got here. He could be anybody's!"

Brian spoke to his son, "We'll go into town and place an ad in the paper. If no one replies in three weeks, you can keep him."

Three weeks! Dave thought his dad was crazy. Surely someone would claim him in three weeks! He knew he had better not argue with his father, though, or it would be a month or more before he could keep him, or worse yet, not be able to keep him at all.

His father's voice interrupted his thoughts. "Why don't you go to the barn and get Rosemary's halter, they look about the same size. We'll see just how much handling this guy's had."

Dave turned to go. "Okay. I'll be right back." He jogged the quarter mile or so to the barn, hoping that the stallion would not take off before he got back. He knew that his father would want to have him gelded if he did stay on the ranch with them, but wondered what he would think about possibly letting him produce a foal with one of the Quarter Horse mares before that happened.

With this thought in mind, he reached the barn and strode in through the doorway. He was big for his age. He had just turned fourteen the month before and he was already almost as tall as his dad. He walked to the hook that had the name "Rosemary" printed carefully above it, grabbed the halter off of it, picked up a nearby lead rope and dashed back out the door. On his way back to the stallion and his father, he saw Rosemary standing in the pasture and yelled, "We're borrowing your halter for a minute, girl!" She watched him disappear over a hill.

When he returned, he found his father petting Snake almost the same way he used to pet Bullet. Dave walked up quietly and Brian put his hand down and took the halter from Dave. Very slowly and quietly, he rubbed it along Snake's neck and then held it in front of his nose, letting him smell it. Snake knew what halters were by now and had no reaction. Brian gently slipped it over the horse's head and secured it. Then, taking the lead rope from Dave, he attached it onto the clip at the bottom of the halter. The horse remained calm and seemed to enjoy their company. Satisfied, he handed the rope to Dave.

As he began to lead Snake, Dave felt absolutely certain that this horse had been handled before; there was no resistance whatsoever. A prairie hen flew up from a ditch beside them, startling Dave a little. Snake didn't jump at all.

"Dad," Dave began, "I think this horse has lived on the prairies or in the wild. That hen didn't scare him in the least."

"I know, I noticed that, too. I thought he might be a wild one from the very start. He has the same features Bullet had." A faraway look came into Brian's eyes. How he had loved that big, handsome horse! He'd raised it from a colt when its mother had been killed by the huge mountain lion that was still lurking around in the hills somewhere.

Dave led Snake to the barn, where he guided him into the new stall that their carpenter, Tony, had just recently completed. He went to the loft ladder, side-stepping Persia and her kittens on the way, climbed the ladder and picked out the lightest, most sweet-smelling bale of hay he could find. He let it drop to the floor below, descended the ladder, and carried it to Snake's stall. There was an old knife lying on the sill and he picked it up and carefully cut the baling twine, took off two flakes, placed them in the brand new manger and broke them up. Next, he walked over to the feed bin, also made by Tony, and took out a measure of oats. He put these in a bucket and filled another with clean, fresh water from the well pump. He walked back to the stall and placed each bucket into the compartments made especially for them. They fit perfectly; Tony was a good carpenter.

The black horse was breathing comfortably, taking in his new surroundings. He looked at Dave, who spoke to him softly. Then, turning from Dave, he nosed at the hay for a moment and gave a soft whinny. Dave was sure that he would be comfortable for the night and left the barn feeling positive that he would be able to keep the beautiful stallion as his own.

Snake, for his part, felt rather calm. Dave had left the lights on in the barn and he observed his new surroundings. He could hear other animals in the building with him and it helped him to relax. He thought about his parents and of all of his friends in the wild band of mustangs that had once been his family. He thought of Paula and the other humans who had been kind to him. He tasted some of the oats that Dave had left for him and relaxed.

The next morning, Dave and Brian went to the office of the local paper. They walked through the big double doors and to the front desk. Behind it sat a small man with thick glasses, poring over a stack of papers. Although he was already balding, Dave could tell that he was not very old.

"May I be of any assistance?" the man asked.

Brian said, "We would like to place an ad in your paper. Could you please tell us where to go?"

The little man looked annoyed. "Well, you can't get lost in this place." It was clear that he was dissatisfied with the office location. "Heck, even if they just ..."

Brian was beginning to get angry. "Could you please just tell us who to see?"

The man looked at him for a long second, as if in a daze. He gave his head a quick shake, apparently trying to rid himself of it, and pointed to a door across the room. "Over there. Knock first." He then went back to his work.

They walked to the door and before Brian had a chance to knock, the doorknob turned and the door opened. They were greeted by a middle-aged woman who looked a bit embarrassed.

"I heard," she said quietly. "I must apologize for Robert." She nodded toward the man at the desk and gestured for them to enter the room. "He's been having a rough day. I'm sorry."

"Thank you, ma'am," said Brian.

"My name is Olivia Sheraton and I'll be happy to assist you with an advertisement. Please sit down."

Brian explained to Olivia the reason that they were there and between the three of them, they had everything worked out in less than ten minutes. The ad would begin to run the following day in the "Lost and Found" section, and would run for three weeks. Olivia bid them farewell and Robert even managed a smile as they left the building.

They decided to stop at their favorite restaurant for lunch while they were in town. While they ordered and ate, they talked about the newly-found horse that fascinated them both equally. Dave told his father of his plans to train him using the techniques that he'd learned about through the countless books that he'd read and from watching experienced handlers on the surrounding properties. Brian listened to his son intently and was proud to see such determination to accomplish something so grand. In his mind, he hoped that there would be no response to the ad that they had just placed with Olivia Sheraton's help. They finished lunch and headed home.

That night, Snake became anxious and began to fuss in his stall. He was very uneasy and felt the need to get out immediately. Confused, he began to kick violently at the enclosure. The other animals in the barn reacted to the noise and there was a flurry of activity among them as well.

The walls of the stalls were solidly built and did not give in to the force of his thrusting legs. He didn't know why, but he knew he had to get out. Stepping back for a moment, he eyed the door through which he had entered the stall. Somehow, he knew that it was his only chance of escape. Moving forward with great force, he slammed his broad chest into the door. The force of the hit stung and he heard a small *snap!* The door did not move. Backing up, he charged at the door again and hit it squarely with his chest, ignoring the pain. There was a sharp cracking sound from the sturdy wood and the other animals in the barn expressed their objections to the commotion, becoming increasingly upset. The chickens, which had been calmly dozing in the aisle, scurried outside to avoid the noise. Many of the other horses craned their necks over their own doors to try to determine exactly what was happening.

Snake again lunged at the door and made solid contact with his shoulder, producing more damage to the hardware holding it in place. Turning around quickly, he gave a mighty kick with his rear legs and one of the hinges actually popped off, flew across the aisle, and hit the stone wall on the other side with a shrill *ping* before falling to the earthen floor.

He stopped, breathing heavily. After a moment, he rammed the door again and there was an enormous *crunch* as the door broke away from its frame and landed with a thud on the floor. Still not even knowing why he felt the need to escape, he just stood there, looking at his handiwork. Once his breathing had returned to a normal rate, he quietly stepped past the battered door and into the aisle. Looking to his right, he saw the darkness outside and trotted to the main doorway. The rest of the horses watched in curious wonder as he exited the barn and disappeared into the night.

~~~~~

It felt good to be outside. The night was warm and quiet. Although the terrain was ever-changing and sometimes challenging, Snake traveled at a steady pace and covered great distances in good time, stopping only to rest and graze from time to time. The chattering of the nighttime animals calmed him and he moved along the landscape with graceful ease.

He still felt as though he were being summoned to some unknown destination and continued moving in roughly the same direction throughout the night. The moon was almost half full in the clear sky and the pale light helped to guide his passage, especially when his footing was made more difficult by rough terrain.

Shortly ahead of him, he could see what appeared to be a creek bed, and as he approached it, he could hear the water gently flowing over the flat rocks in the stream. Reaching it, he stretched his long neck down and took a cool drink. He had covered many miles since his departure from the York's property and felt secure enough in this location to

take a short nap. Resting beside the stream, he dozed off
and dreamed of his lost friends.

When he awoke a short time later, the sun was just
beginning to peek over the horizon. The crickets had
stopped their chirping sing-song and the dew was sparkling
on the green grass all around him. He gazed ahead and
prepared to begin another leg of his journey to the
unknown. After taking a drink, he grazed and then began
moving in the same direction that he had been traveling the
night before. He was being called by something unknown
to him, but there didn't seem to be any question that he was
moving in the right direction. He would have another day
of good progress and by the time the sun began its descent
in the sky late that afternoon, he found himself tired, but
feeling good about his progress.

The ground was flatter here, making travel easier for
him. He was walking through a field of wildflowers when
he heard a soft whinny, stopping him in his tracks. Looking
in the direction from which it had come, he saw a stallion
and three small mares. The gentle breeze blew their scent
to him, even though they were a good distance away. They
did not see him. Standing perfectly still, he watched as they
grazed contentedly.

He had not expected this, and was not sure what to do.
Not knowing these horses, he did not know how they would
react to him, especially the stallion. He was very lonely,
but he knew that this could be trouble. Not moving a
muscle, he kept an eye on the stallion, who obviously had
no idea that there was any other horse nearby. Snake knew
that he needed to make a choice before his presence became
known.

He knew that he must continue his lonesome journey.
The sense of calling that he had been feeling seemed to
overpower any urge to fight for these mares. He silently
watched the four horses as they calmly nibbled on the grass,

their scents filling his nose and again reminding him of his greatly missed friends.

Only about fifty yards ahead of him was a wooded area. It would be good cover and put an end to the miserable situation in which he had found himself. Barely turning his head, he eyed the stallion and the distance to the woods. He would need to be quiet, but fast at the same time.

He waited until the stallion was facing away from him and bolted. Never looking back, he galloped toward the trees. Once inside the stand of trees, he kept his speed up as much as he could while maneuvering around the majestic growth. It was much darker and cooler among the trees and he pricked his ears up, listening for any sound behind him, while at the same time making amazing forward progress. Scrambling to avoid any low-hanging branches and sometimes having to leap over fallen trees, he was exhausted and finally slowed to a trot, still listening intently.

Except for the angry birds that he had disturbed, he heard nothing. His sides were heaving and his nostrils flared. He stood in the shadows of the trees and strained every one of his senses to pinpoint any sign of danger.

He was alone with the fluttering birds. He realized that he had just taken himself away from what might have been the best thing that could have happened to him. He thought about the stallion and felt sure that he could have easily overpowered him for the sake of the mares, but he was still being compelled to continue his journey through the countryside. He breathed a heavy sigh and began walking.

~~~~~

The black Mustang rumbled steadily along the unpaved road. The ditches on either side of the roadway were still soggy from the recent rain. Tyler Tucker turned up the music on the radio and sang along.

The long trip had gone very well and he was almost home with his prized old car. Tyler had been waiting to obtain the major parts to get restoration of the car started. It had taken several months, but he felt that he was ready to begin the process. He had most of the parts he needed with a little cash left over for any unforeseen problems. Luckily, the engine had been agreeable and there'd been no mechanical problems along the way. His plan was to restore the old Mustang to its former glory.

Tyler had purchased the car from his older cousin, Steve, who had had it since it was brand new. Over the years, Steve had taken excellent care of the car, but it had a lot of miles on it. Tyler remembered the car from when, as a small boy, his family would go to visit Steve and his family. He had always loved it and never dreamed that he would some day own it. Steve had tired of the car and chosen, instead, to buy newer vehicles almost every year. The car had been stored in their barn for several years. Steve would start the car and let it run every few months, but it hadn't been on the road in a long time. Tyler had taken care of the paperwork and licensing following the sale and now he only needed to get it back to his shop, where the real work would begin.

He was on the final leg of the long drive home, but he would still be on the dirt road for at least another half hour. He had always lived in the country and wouldn't have it any other way; he knew that he wouldn't see a single house or another human being for miles and miles. Ever since the county had built the new highway, the old dirt road was seldom, if ever, used by anyone. Tyler preferred the longer drive in the country over having to deal with the traffic and people who didn't know how to drive.

He wanted to get home before dark, if possible. He knew that his wife would have all of their horses brought in and fed by the time he got there, but one of the geldings had been having trouble with a skin condition on his chest and he really wanted to check it out before morning. He had been treating it himself for the past week, trying to get it cleared up to avoid having to call the vet out to have a look at him.

Tyler accelerated and enjoyed the car's response. He was impressed with its running condition and the good time he'd made getting home.

The buck was out of the weeds and sailing over the roadside ditch before Tyler even knew what it was. At the moment before impact, he could see the indignant surprise and confusion in its big eyes and there was a sound like wet sandbags hitting the car at the right headlight. Tyler was propelled into the steering wheel, wrenching the tires to the left and sending the car to the other side of the road, sliding sideways and throwing chunks of dirt and stones into the air. As it left the roadway, the front tires spun crazily before the car hit the far side of the ditch, teetered for a moment, and came to a lopsided rest at the bottom.

~~~~~~~

Snake was still traveling alone. He had covered a great distance and was in remarkably good shape. The weather had been relatively nice and he was faring well physically. He was a strong horse with good instincts and he knew that he was on course. He moved with a desire to *be* where he needed to be and *do* what he needed to do.

There had been no more encounters and he finally seemed to be slowing down. In his mind, there was no more need to push forward with the same sense of urgency that he had felt before. He had just taken a good roll in the mud and the heat of the day was beginning to wane when he heard it.

"Ahh..."

He stopped. Listened. He heard no sound; the evening was silent. Even the birds seemed to be absent. Shaking himself lightly, he readied himself to continue traveling when he heard it again.

"Oohhh"

It wasn't threatening, and he thought it was the sound of a man. He stood still, waiting to hear it again. He thought about all the men that he had known. He thought about Paula and the sweet apples. He thought about his lost band. And still, it was quiet. He heard nothing.

He began to make his way out of the thick vegetation when he heard a *click ... thud*, followed by an "Ugh!"

What was going on?

Again, there was silence. He continued forward and his nose began to burn. Something was not right. Ahead of him, he could see the trees beginning to break, and, summoning up his strength for what could be in store, he bravely continued his path.

His curiosity had also kicked in by now. He walked slowly, carefully listening for anything that would tell him who or what was making the sounds. As he walked, the trees gradually became less dense and the shadows turned to light. It was as he was stepping over a fallen branch that he first saw the black car in the ditch. He stopped immediately and looked curiously at the sight before him.

The car was perched at an angle and one of the doors was partially open. A man sat inside, slowly rubbing one side of his face. Snake stood as still as a statue, watching, waiting to see what would happen. The man was still moaning now and then, and Snake knew that he was hurt. The man made no attempt to get out of the car.

Snake stood there silently. Somehow he knew that this man was no threat to him, injured or not. Suddenly, he remembered the smoke, could almost smell it as he stood there. He remembered the gripping pain on his leg and he was once again that young horse, unable to get free of the trap. In his mind, he was there again. He knew who this man was!

He remembered, and he knew what he had to do.

~~~~~~

Tyler knew something in his foot was broken. He didn't know how long he'd been on the side of the road, but already the swelling was creating immense pressure inside his boot. He'd have to get it off his foot. He slid over toward the door that he'd managed to get partway open and twisted his body to the right. With great effort, he was able to lift his leg up and onto the passenger seat. With his foot throbbing, he unlaced his boot. There was still daylight left, but he didn't put much hope in seeing anyone who would be traveling along the desolate stretch of road. He supposed that his best chance would be to crawl.

He removed the lace completely from the boot, pulled the tongue out and opened up the leather boot as much as possible. Pulling his foot toward his body and firmly grasping the boot with both hands, he closed his eyes and pulled the heel away from his body, ignoring the pain. The worn boot slid off easily and he did not see any blood on the sock. He rested, trying to will the throbbing to stop. He had to get out of the car and up onto the road as quickly as possible. Looking out the window, he could see that the door had been prevented from opening any further by a mound of earth and rocks. The car was leaning to the left and he didn't see much chance of getting the other door open and exiting out the other side.

He grabbed the small bag of cookies lying on the seat and shoved them down the back of his shirt. Turning over onto his front, he angled his body and squeezed head first out of the opening with little room to spare. Getting any kind of grip on the wet earth was almost impossible and his progress was very slow. Inching forward, he smelled gasoline and heard a steady *splat, splat, splat*. Pushing with his knees as best he could, and grabbing onto the most solid pieces of ground that he could see, he moved slowly forward until his feet were resting on the edge of the car. Pushing against the ground with his good leg and trying desperately to keep the injured foot in the air, he made the final effort to remove himself completely from the car. His booted foot hit the ground with a soft thud and he waited a moment before gently allowing the other one to come to rest on the soft earth.

"Ahhh!" he whispered.

His clothing was already soaked through to the skin. He needed to rest. The removal of the boot had relieved a lot of the pressure on his foot, but the throbbing pain was relentless. Resting his head on his folded arms in front of him, he tried not to think about what was about to happen. He thought of his wife and wondered how long she would wait before she came looking for him. He had not given her any specific time to expect him back and he knew that his only option was to get himself out of the ditch and back up onto the road.

As he lay there, there was movement in the woods just beyond the ditch and he heard the distinctive snap of a fallen branch cracking under the weight of something heavy.

What? What now? Am I really going to die here?

Tyler tried to remain calm as he heard whatever was making its way through the woods come closer to him. He didn't remember ever feeling so helpless in all his life. He closed his eyes and said a quick prayer and that was when he heard the nicker. A nicker! Daring to open his eyes, he adjusted to the fading light and saw a dirty horse standing at the edge of the woods looking directly at him.

"Hey, buddy," he croaked. His throat was dry. He

dropped his head back onto his arms. Lying beside the car, he could still hear tiny drops of gasoline hitting the waterlogged dirt.

The thought occurred to him that if there was a horse out here, there could certainly be someone with it. He raised his head again and looked at the horse, which stood watching him intently. "Hey!" he yelled. "Is anybody there?" The horse snorted and gently pawed at the ground. There was no other sound. "Hey! Hello?" All he heard were the crickets beginning their nightly chorus, the soft breathing of the horse, and the sound of the gas dripping. It was time to go.

He raised himself up on his arms and tried to see beyond the car. From his viewpoint, it looked like the best way back up to the road would be to go in front of the car. It appeared to be slightly less muddy and a shorter distance, as well. Lowering onto his elbows, he scooted to the right, causing a shot of pain from his foot and up his entire right side, making his fingers tingle. He slumped back down onto the ground, completely deflated.

The horse nickered again and shook itself. Tyler could hear small pieces of dried mud hitting the ground where the horse stood.

"Ahhh, God help me," he said softly. He scanned the ground, looking for something that he could use as a crutch. Rather than crawling on his hands and knees, a good, solid branch might allow him to make faster time once he was back onto the road.

The horse began to move, stepping very slowly. It lowered its head and watched Tyler as it neared. Its ears were alert and Tyler could have sworn that the horse had an expression of sympathy in its eyes.

He watched as it came closer and navigated down the side of the ditch until it was standing directly beside him in the awful trench. Tyler blinked his eyes and looked at the hooves just a couple feet from his battered body. The horse gave a small whinny, turned around, moved slightly to the right, and lowered itself down onto its front legs. Turning its head to the left and keeping an eye on its distance from Tyler, it gently lowered its full weight onto the ground, keeping its legs neatly folded beside its body.

Tyler, for his part, was so astounded that he watched the movements of the animal without a sound or a single movement. The stallion was now lying beside him in the ditch!

He reached his hand out and touched the horse. The stallion shook his head slightly and turned to look at him. There seemed to be a connection between the two of them. Tyler made no other movement and the horse snorted and shook its head again. *Let's go!* it seemed to be saying.

Tyler was worn out and having trouble understanding exactly what was happening. Was this horse asking him to get on its back? If it was, he wasn't sure he had the strength, and even if he did manage, how could he be sure that he wouldn't be injured further if this was not the horse's intention?

Daylight was quickly disappearing and Tyler knew that he had to make a decision. His hand still rested on the horse and he moved it gently down its side. The horse drew in a deep breath and sighed, seemingly out of patience, although it made no effort to get up.

"Where'd you come from?" Tyler said quietly. The horse turned to look at him and made no reply.

Having learned to ride at the age of four, Tyler was an experienced horseman. He knew the unpredictability of a wild mustang, which this horse certainly appeared to be. With his situation being what it was, though, it was hard to convince himself not to take a chance on allowing the horse to help him, as it seemed to want to do.

Wincing in pain, he shifted his weight, pulled his legs up to his body and got the ball of his good left foot solidly on the ground. The horse remained perfectly still as he pushed off the ground, clutched its mane in his hands, and pulled his body up until he was lying on top of it. The horse whinnied softly, nodded its head, and then they were both motionless as Tyler rested. After a few moments, he took a deep breath and slowly raised his right leg up and over the back of the horse, pivoting his body to face the front. This action started the throbbing again, and he winced in pain as he slowly let his leg slide down the other side of the horse and rested the back of his foot on the ground as gently as he could. He was now straddling this amazing animal, which had remained calm. He reached his arm out to its neck and patted it reassuringly.

"Good boy .... thank you," he murmured. The horse twitched its ears and Tyler could hear the soft swish of its tail behind him.

For a moment, he wondered if it was possible that he was still sitting in the car, unconscious, and simply dreaming all of this, but the intense pain in his foot and the heat generating from this magnificent animal made him realize, without question, that it *was* really happening.

He continued to talk softly to the horse as they became accustomed to each other. At the same time, he inspected the terrain of the ditch more closely from his new position. The side leading up to the road wasn't too much of an incline and he felt sure that the horse would have no problem climbing it. He placed his hands on either side of the horse's withers, leaned down, scooted himself forward and laid the side of his head on the horse's neck. Patting it gently, he spoke to it. "Come on, buddy ... let's get outta here." The horse continued to astonish him by slowly getting to its feet.

He had no idea how he was going to maneuver their progress. Riding bareback was one thing, but riding bareback with no bridle was something else entirely. If this didn't work out, he guessed that he could always dismount onto his good foot (hopefully) and resort back to his first plan of crawling or searching for something that he could use as a crutch.

The stallion, however, seemed to have his own thoughts and took the first step up the grade of the ditch. Tyler was still leaning forward against the horse's neck, his left hand clutching the thick mane and his right arm wrapped against the horse's body, ensuring that he would keep his seat. The horse was out of the ditch in seconds and standing on the road in the fading twilight.

"Good boy," he said. "Stay on the road ... okay? Can you do that?" He patted the horse's shoulder and sat up straight. The night was quiet and he looked into the sky. The moon, just beginning its customary advance through the sky, was a little more than half full. Except for some scattered clouds, the sky was clear and Tyler guessed that they would probably have decent light.

The horse nickered and seemed to be considering its next move. Tyler, while knowing better than to expect another miracle, very gently pressed his right leg against the horse's body; they needed to make a slight turn to the left in order to follow the road toward home. The horse made no response.

"Come on, buddy. Let's take a walk."

The horse stood still. Tyler sighed. He was exhausted. He thought about his wife and wondered if she had left the house to look for him. She would have no way of knowing that he had chosen to take the old dirt road rather than the new county road that everyone else seemed to prefer; most people were not even aware that this road was still open to traffic. He listened to the crickets and breathed in the distinct smell of the animal. It wasn't long before the horse nickered softly and began to move.

~~~~~

Snake was happy that the man had finally understood that he wanted to help. He knew that the man was hurt and that he had to get him to people. They would be able to help the man, just as the man had once helped him. He understood that he needed to change his usual ways of avoiding people. He had to find someone, and he knew from experience that his chances would be much better if he stayed on this long, flat stretch of treeless land.

He kept his pace steady, his hooves thudding softly on the old dirt road. The man on his back was very still and mostly quiet, except for times when he would speak softly and pat his neck or shoulder. The night was very still and Snake continued to listen intently for any sounds that could be attributed to people. He too, was getting tired. A small black and white cat had appeared from somewhere and was silently following them. Together, the three of them continued along the dark road.

~~~~~

In the moonglow, Tyler checked his watch again and saw that they had been traveling for almost three hours. In the soft moonlight, he thought he saw a turn in the road ahead of them. He blinked when he saw what appeared to be lights peeping through the thick trees and vegetation straight ahead. *Was there a house in the distance?* He didn't remember any residences in this area.

Suddenly, he remembered reading about the old furniture factory that had been closed for years. When was it due to reopen? He couldn't remember, but he was almost positive that this would be the right location. The small, family-owned factory was located off a paved road which ran parallel to the dirt road ahead, with at least a mile between

68

them, he guessed. The only way to reach it would be through the woods. How could he expect the horse to change its course? It had been following the road since they'd begun.

His mind spun as he considered his options. The old dirt road would not bring them to any populated area for miles. He was exhausted and it was obvious that the horse was also becoming tired. Tyler needed to continue going straight ahead at the turn, into the trees, and head for the lights. He needed to get off the road!

~~~~~

Snake saw the lights, too. He thought there might be people around them, people who would give help to the man on his back. He whinnied and quickened his pace.

The man was talking more now and Snake could tell that he was sitting up straighter. As they approached the sharp turn in the road, the man talked almost non stop, patting Snake on the neck and seemingly becoming excited. He thought the man also saw the lights.

When they came to the section of the road that began to turn to the left, Snake slowed his pace, peering into the darkness of the dense growth. He continued forward in the same direction and stopped only briefly at the edge of the ditch beside the road before stepping down and into it. He could feel the man lean forward, press his body against the base of his neck, and pull his arms snug against his body as he climbed up and out the other side.

Stepping on the soft ground beside the ditch, Snake stopped and looked into the trees. He could smell the sweet dampness of the growth as he stood just outside of it. The man patted his neck and spoke to him. As he began to step forward into the tall trees, the cat sat down on the road, wrapped its tail tightly around itself, and watched them disappear into the darkness.

~~~~~

Tyler could feel the temperature drop as they entered the thick stand of trees. It felt wonderful and revived his senses. He looked ahead as the horse made its way among the trees and the undergrowth, but saw no sign of the lights. As long as he could keep his sense of direction, he thought they would be okay.

They continued forward, slowly, and the growth of the trees became much more dense. After getting thwacked in the face several times by low-hanging branches, Tyler decided it was best to keep his head down. Once again, he leaned forward and hugged the horse.

The moonlight was lost beneath the trees, but Tyler could feel that the horse was not hindered much, as it made its way slowly through the uneven terrain. He could hear the sounds of the woods and small animals scurrying away from their path.

The horse made his way expertly through the trees and after some time Tyler heard the sound of running water and realized again how thirsty he was. The horse was keeping a steady pace, but Tyler was sure that he heard it, too; there was a creek not far away. Listening and looking around, he could make out a glimmer of moving water just ahead of them. From what he could see from his seat, it was not wide or deep and would not be an obstacle for them.

The horse came to the stream and stopped. After glancing back at Tyler, it lowered its head and took a long drink. Tyler sat on the horse and longed for some water. His throat felt like dryer lint and he had to stop himself from sliding off the horse and burying his face in the cool water.

"Have some for me," he managed to mutter to his mount, and stroked his neck.

The horse lifted its head and stood for several minutes, resting.

Tyler listened. It was late at night, but still he listened. He thought that by now they must be getting close to their target. He wanted to hear the sound of a car. Anything.

He looked through the trees, trying to see the lights that they had seen from the road. He twisted his body, rising up as far as he could, trying to see from every angle, but saw nothing through the thick foliage. He felt sure, still, that they were moving in the right direction and tried to relax for a moment with the horse.

"Let me know when you're ready, big guy."

Suddenly, he felt as if he were on the verge of tears. He was so tired and thirsty. His foot hurt. He had a bag of cookies plastered to his back that he couldn't even eat. He slumped forward onto the horse and quietly wept as it began to step into the water.

They continued into the darkness. The horse did not seem to mind when Tyler would squeeze his knees together and raise his body up to try to see what was ahead. Pushing leaves and branches away as they went, he looked and listened, ducking when necessary.

He had just raised his body after they had gotten past a particularly nasty tree when Tyler saw the twinkle of a light. It was off to the right of them, but it was there. He saw it. They were still well within the woods, but he thought if the horse kept going relatively straight, they would absolutely get to the road.

"Come on, buddy, we're almost there."

Tyler spoke softly to the horse, and, even in the darkness, he could see its ears move to the sound of his voice. He could almost *feel* the horse listening to him.

It was at that moment that Tyler sensed the open sky

trying to show itself. The moonlight was still struggling through the trees, but he knew that they were almost out of the woods. He could see the glow of lights through the leaves of the trees and he ran his fingers through the horse's thick mane.

"My buddy."

They were both so exhausted that they almost stumbled over the guardrail. Tyler slid forward as the horse drew up its right front leg and stopped. Tyler looked at the road and was surprised to see it. Looking to his left, he saw a dark curve in the roadway and to his right he could see the source of the light.

Standing some distance off the other side of the road was the tiny factory. Tyler hadn't seen it in years and it looked sort of eerie, even under the circumstances. He could see a white work truck parked in front of the main building, but he didn't see any movement. The horse was very still. Tyler knew that he was tired, too. He leaned forward and spoke to the horse.

"Hey, buddy, I'm gonna have to yell, okay?"

The horse twitched an ear and stood still.

"Hey!" Tyler tried to shout. It came out muffled and dry. He cleared his throat, twice, and saw a young man come out of the building.

"Hey! Help!" he croaked.

The horse shook its head. Tyler tried to swallow and clear his throat when the horse raised its head and neighed. Once, twice, three times.

Tyler saw the man look in their direction.

"Hey! Can you help me?"

The horse neighed again and discovered that it could make noise by tapping its hoof against the metal guardrail.

"Hey!"

The man stopped walking and continued to look in their direction.

"Hey! Please help!"

72

The horse became quiet as the man walked toward them.

"Who's there?" he asked.

"Please. Do you have a phone?" Tyler replied in a rasp. "I need a doctor. Can you call my wife?"

The man was still walking toward them, obviously unable to see them in the darkness.

"Who's there?" he repeated.

"We need help. Please," Tyler pleaded.

The young man was crossing the road.

"Do you have any water?"

The man stopped and looked at them.

"Are you okay?" he asked.

"I need a phone. Can you call my wife? I need a doctor."

The young man stood looking at them for a long moment before he replied, "Yeah, there's a phone in there. Wow. Are you okay?"

"My foot's messed up. Can you call my wife?" he repeated.

The man reached into his shirt pocket and pulled out a pen.

"What's her number?"

Tyler recited their phone number and, in the moonlight, the young man wrote it on the back of his hand.

"What's her name?" he asked Tyler.

"Penny," Tyler replied, hoping that she would be home. "Can you bring me some water, please? And ask her to bring a halter and one of the trailers, okay?"

"No problem. I'll be back in a sec." He turned and trotted across the road toward the building.

While they waited for him to return, Tyler leaned forward again and rested his head along the horse's neck. He could feel that the horse was relaxed and he said a silent prayer of thanks for having found the kid there so late. Several minutes passed before he heard the young man approaching them.

"Wow," he repeated. "Five more minutes and I would have been gone. Your wife's on her way. I didn't really know what to tell her, but she knows where you're at." He reached over the guardrail and handed Tyler a bottle of water.

"Thanks," Tyler said gratefully. He opened the bottle and drank almost half of it before he lowered it and rested it on his thigh. "I really needed that." He gave the young man a quick version of what had happened and how they'd ended up there.

"Wow," said the young man when Tyler had finished. "I'm glad I was still here! I had to finish up some things for an inspection on Monday," he said, gesturing across the road toward the buildings. "They're gonna open back up over there."

Tyler nodded. He was so tired. "Is she gonna bring a trailer?"

"Yeah," the young man replied. "She said you don't really need another horse," he added, laughing.

"She'll change her mind," Tyler replied, smiling, and the two men continued to talk until Penny arrived.

*****

Dear Reader,

Thank you for reading *Meeting of the Mustangs*. If you enjoyed it, I'd appreciate it if you could take a moment to leave a short review and tell your friends about it. Word of mouth is an indie author's best friend.
You can find me on Facebook or feel free to send any questions or comments that you may have. I would love to hear from you at tuxcats@yahoo.com!

Sincerely,

Cathy Kennedy

Made in the USA
Middletown, DE
31 March 2023

27986830R10046